Weekly Reader Presents

Boober Fraggle's Giant Wish

By Jocelyn Stevenson • Pictures by Jeffrey Severn

Muppet Press
Henry Holt and Company
NEW YORK

Weekly Reader Books offers several exciting
card and activity programs. For information,
write to WEEKLY READER BOOKS, P.O. Box 16636,
Columbus, Ohio 43216.

This book is a presentation of
Weekly Reader Books.

Weekly Reader Books offers book clubs for children
from preschool through high school.

For further information write to:
Weekly Reader Books
4343 Equity Drive
Columbus, Ohio 43228

Weekly Reader is a trademark of Field Publications.

Library of Congress Cataloging in Publication Data

Stevenson, Jocelyn.
Boober Fraggle's giant wish.
Summary: A magic wishing fork grants Boober's wish
to be as big as Junior Gorg.
[1. Size—Fiction. 2. Puppets—Fiction] I. Severn,
Jeffrey, ill. II. Title.
PZ7.S8476Bq 1986 [E] 86-4635
ISBN: 0-8050-0068-2
Printed in the United States of America

BOOBER Fraggle peeked out of the tunnel. He was worried. "How am I supposed to get to the Trash Heap when a big Gorg is waiting out there to thump me?"

Boober desperately needed some information, and the all-seeing, all-knowing Trash Heap was always happy to tell a Fraggle like Boober anything he needed to know. The problem was that the Trash Heap lived in the gigantic Gorgs' gigantic Garden.

Boober started to walk up and down the tunnel, muttering nervously. "When the Trash Heap gave me the recipe for onion-skin stew, she forgot to say how many onion skins to use." Boober kept thinking about his hungry friends, who were waiting for him to finish his stew. "Oh, this is terrible!" he moaned.

Just then, the enormous eye of Junior Gorg peered into the hole. "You still in there, Fraggle?" boomed Junior.

Boober was so scared his stomach felt as if he'd swallowed a boulder, and his heart was thumping so hard he could barely breathe.

As Boober felt his legs collapse beneath him, he heard a voice calling, "Junior!" It was Junior Gorg's mother. "I need your help, oh Prince of the Universe."

"In a minute, Ma," answered Junior.

Ma Gorg put her hands on her hips. "Junior, remember what happens to young Gorgs who don't do as they're told?"

"Yes, Ma," Junior answered with a sigh. "The Do-As-You're-Told Monster comes and chases them around the garden. But that's just a silly old story." Still, Junior lumbered off toward the castle just in case.

The minute Junior was safely out of sight, Boober ducked out of the tunnel and bolted toward the Trash Heap.

"Oh, Madam Heap," panted Boober, forgetting all about the onion-skin stew. "Being scared of Gorgs is so bad for my health! It makes my stomach hurt and my heart go BAM BAM BAM. I wish I were bigger—huge even! Then I wouldn't have to be so scared."

"I've got just the thing," said the Trash Heap. She rummaged noisily through her tin cans and orange rinds and pulled up an old fork. "This is a magic wishing fork," she declared, handing it to Boober. "Whatever you wish while holding it will come true. But at sundown, you must return the fork to me. I need it to eat my supper. So, if you have to unwish a wish, do it by sundown. Otherwise, whatever you wish sticks. Forever." With that, the Trash Heap yawned and slowly sank into the leaves.

As Boober walked back toward Fraggle Rock, he thought of all the different wishes he could make. He was thinking so hard that he didn't see Junior Gorg. But Junior Gorg saw him.

"Fraggle!" shouted Junior.

Boober froze. Then he clutched the magic fork harder. "I . . . I wish I were as big as you," he whispered.

The next thing Boober knew, his wish had come true.

"It worked!" Boober gasped, looking at Junior eye to eye. "I'm as big as the Gorg!"

Junior Gorg stared back at Boober. At first he looked puzzled. Then he looked surprised. Then he looked downright scared. "Oh, no!" he shouted. "I-i-i-it's the Do-As-You're-Told Monster!"

Meanwhile, back at Fraggle Rock, Gobo, Mokey, Red,
and Wembley were waiting for their friend Boober to return.
"What's taking him so long?" asked Red, rubbing her
stomach. "I'm starving."

"Maybe we ought to go find out if he needs help,"
suggested Mokey.
"Well, if it's the fastest way to get dinner, let's go!" said Gobo.
So the four Fraggles set off toward the Gorgs' Garden.

When they got to the opening to the Garden, Gobo
peeked outside.

"Look!" he shouted.

The other Fraggles crowded around the hole.

"Is that Boober?" asked Mokey. She couldn't believe her eyes.

"He's huge!" said Red.

"He's chasing the Gorg!" yelped Wembley.

Boober's shocked friends sneaked into the Garden to get a better look. Gobo sat down on a hard object sticking out of the ground. "I *wish* we knew what was going on," he muttered.

Suddenly, they all knew the whole story. That's because Gobo was sitting on the magic wishing fork. Boober had dropped it after he made his big wish.

"Boober!" his friends all shouted together. "The magic
wishing fork! It's right here! Wish yourself back to your
old size before it's too late!"

Red pointed to the sky. It was almost sundown.

Boober turned and saw his friends waving their arms and pointing to the fork. They looked very, very tiny.

"I don't want to be small again!" he called down to them. "When I was small, I was scared of everything! It wasn't healthy! But that's all different now!" He turned to Junior. "Hey, Gorg! I'm not scared of you!"

Junior just crawled under the wheelbarrow. "Oh, Mr. Do-As-You're-Told Monster, I promise I'll always do as I'm told. Honest!"

Boober's friends were becoming more and more worried as the sun sank lower and lower.

"Boober! If you don't wish yourself small soon, you'll have to stay out here forever!" shouted Mokey.

"Where will you sleep?" cried Wembley.

"Come back and finish your stew!" called Red.

Boober wasn't listening. He was too busy being big. "Well, Gorg, now you know how we little Fraggles feel when you big Gorgs chase us," he said.

Junior peeked out from behind the wheelbarrow. "Wait a minute. You mean you're a Fraggle?" he asked. "I thought you were the Do-As-You're-Told Monster."

"No, I'm a big, brave Fraggle," said Boober proudly.

"But I'm not scared of Fraggles," said Junior.

"Not even a Fraggle who's as b-b-b-big as you?" Boober gulped nervously.

"What's big got to do with it? You're a Fraggle, not a monster. And I love to chase Fraggles, no matter what size they are!" Then Junior Gorg jumped up and lunged toward Boober.

"Boober! The fork!" shouted Gobo as Boober ran past. He stuck the fork under Boober's giant toe.

"Ouch!" roared Boober, hopping up and down. Junior was closing in fast.

"Make a wish!" yelled Red. The sun was almost down.

"I wish I were the size of a Fraggle again!" yelled Boober.

His wish came true. Suddenly, he was his old size again. The five Fraggles raced toward the tunnel. But just then Boober remembered the magic fork. "Oh, no!" he wailed. "I promised I'd get it back to the Trash Heap." Taking a deep breath, he dashed past Junior Gorg, grabbed the fork, and ran as fast as he could.

The Trash Heap was just starting her supper when Boober returned the fork. "So, how did you like being big?" she asked.

"It's just as unhealthy as being small," said Boober, sighing. "Being big doesn't mean you can't be scared."

"True," agreed the Trash Heap. "But being small doesn't mean you can't be brave. You ran back here with my fork even though the Gorg was chasing you. That's what I call brave."

Just then, Boober's friends ran in. "Boober, are you all right?" they all asked at once.

"I guess so," said Boober. "The Trash Heap just said I've been brave."

"Well then, are you brave enough to try my new recipe?" asked the Trash Heap, smiling.

Boober nodded. He closed his eyes and took a big gulp. It was delicious. "Onion-skin stew!" he said.

"With six whole onion skins," added the Trash Heap proudly.

Then Boober, his friends, and the Trash Heap bravely finished every last drop.